DEC 3 - 2007

W9-BMC-698

WITHDRAWN

SOUND WAVES

The Rosen Publishing Group's
PowerKids Press™
New York

Ian F. Mahaney

Published in 2007 by The Rosen Publishing Group, Inc.
29 East 21st Street, New York, NY 10010

First Edition

Editor: Joanne Randolph
Book Design: Julio Gil

Photo Credits: Cover and title page © M. Thomsen/zefa/Corbis; p. 7 © www.istockphoto.com/Tony Svensson; p. 8 © www.istockphoto.com/Galina Barskaya; p. 10 © P. Wilson/zefa/Corbis; pp. 11, 13 adapted from NASA and Science@NASA; p. 12 © www.istockphoto.com/Matt Matthews; p. 15 © www.istockphoto.com/Ian Harvey; p. 16 © Reuters/Corbis; p. 17 © Joe McDonald/Corbis; p. 18 © Jonathan Blair/Corbis; p. 19 © Tom Stewart/Corbis; p. 21 © www.istockphoto.com/Shaun Lowe; pp. 20, 21, 22 Adriana Skura.

Library of Congress Cataloging-in-Publication Data

Mahaney, Ian F.
   Sound waves / Ian F. Mahaney.
      p. cm. — (Energy in action)
   Includes index.
   ISBN (10) 1-4042-3480-2 (13) 978-1-4042-3480-2 (lib. bdg.) —
ISBN (10) 1-4042-2189-1 (13) 978-1-4042-2189-5 (pbk.)
   1. Sound-waves—Juvenile literature. 2. Sound—Juvenile literature. I. Title. II. Energy in action (PowerKids Press)
   QC243.2.M34 2007
   534—dc22
                                                2006001591

Manufactured in the United States of America

CONTENTS

Atoms and Molecules

Everything on Earth and beyond is made up of **matter**. Matter is anything that takes up space. **Atoms** are tiny bits of matter. The air people breathe, rain, and the hair on your head are each made up of an uncountable number of atoms.

Molecules are collections of atoms. Have you ever heard of water described as H_2O? This is because one molecule of water has two hydrogen atoms and one oxygen atom. Hydrogen and oxygen are both gases that you cannot see or smell. Matter is always moving around from place to place. This movement of matter is important to the sounds that we hear every day.

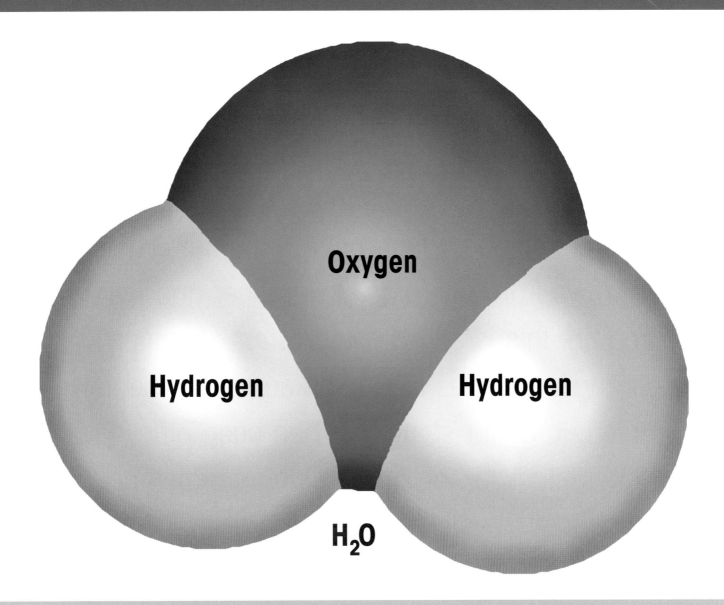

Oxygen

Hydrogen

Hydrogen

H_2O

This is a picture of a water molecule. The blue shape is the oxygen atom. The two gray shapes are the hydrogen atoms. The place where these shapes are joined together is called a bond.

What Is Sound?

When a police car with a loud siren rushes by, we can hear the sound of the siren. Have you ever stopped to think about exactly what sound is, though? Sounds are noises that our ears sense. The noises are created by fast-moving atoms. When atoms move from one place to another and then back again, this is called a **vibration**. Vibrating atoms and molecules create the sound we hear. An example is a guitar string that has been plucked. When it is plucked, the guitar string vibrates and we hear a sound. People use these vibrations to make music on the guitar. In fact sound waves are **energy** that we can hear!

Have you ever heard a church bell ringing? There is a metal piece that hangs from the center of the bell. As the bell swings, this metal part strikes the bell and causes it to vibrate. We hear the vibrations as the bell continues to ring.

Our Vocal Cords

A sound you probably hear every day is people talking. When you talk part of you is vibrating. When people talk they push air through their throats into a part of the throat called the **larynx**. The air passes through a part of the larynx called the **vocal cords**. Our vocal cords vibrate and create sound. If you hold your fingers on your neck while talking or making noise, you can feel your vocal cords vibrating. Try humming or making silly noises. Change the volume of the sounds. Can you feel the vibrations that your vocal cords are making?

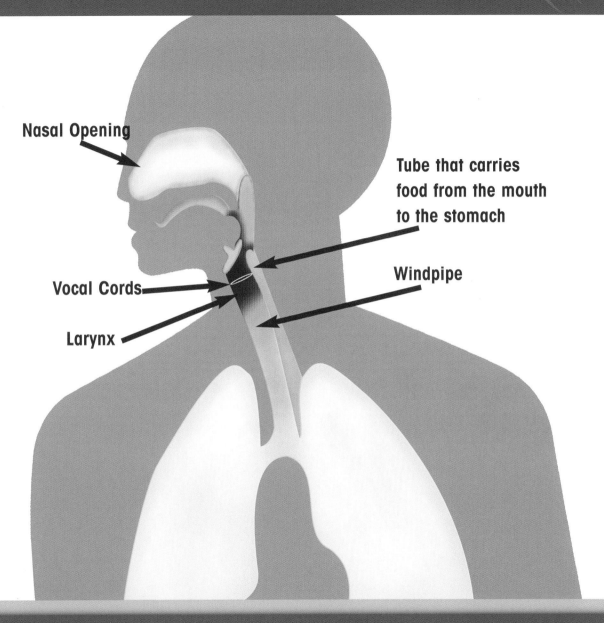

Nasal Opening

Tube that carries food from the mouth to the stomach

Vocal Cords

Windpipe

Larynx

Opposite: These girls are using their vocal cords as they talk to one another. *Above:* This picture shows where the vocal cords and the larynx are. You will feel the vibrations from speech if you hold your fingers right where the underside of your chin meets your neck.

Waves

Have you ever been on a boat and noticed that the boat moves up and down? This is because the water is moving up and down. Water moving in this way is called a wave. Sound moves like this, too, but we cannot see it. Sound waves move up and down like ocean waves. Sound waves also move side to side. If you call your friend's name, the sound waves will travel in an up-and-down and side-to-side motion to your friend's ears.

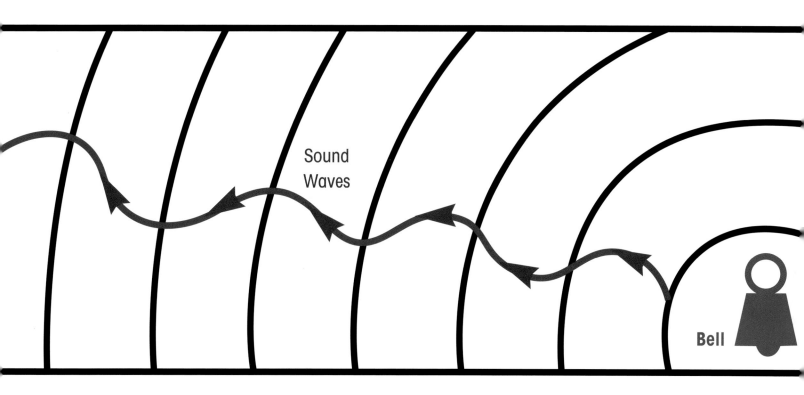

Sound
Waves

Bell

Opposite: Picturing an ocean wave will help you understand what a sound wave is like.
Above: This picture shows that as a bell rings, the waves of sound move outward and away from the bell.

Hearing Sound Waves

The ears of people and other animals have three parts. These parts are the outer ear, the middle ear, and the inner ear. The outer ear is the part we can see. Its job is to collect sounds from outside and pass them through the ear canal to the middle ear. The middle ear includes three small bones called the **hammer**, the **anvil**, and the **stirrup**. These bones vibrate when sound waves reach them. The vibrations are then passed to the inner ear. The inner ear is a combination of tiny hairs and liquid called the **cochlea**. The cochlea **translates** the vibrations into sounds that our brains can understand.

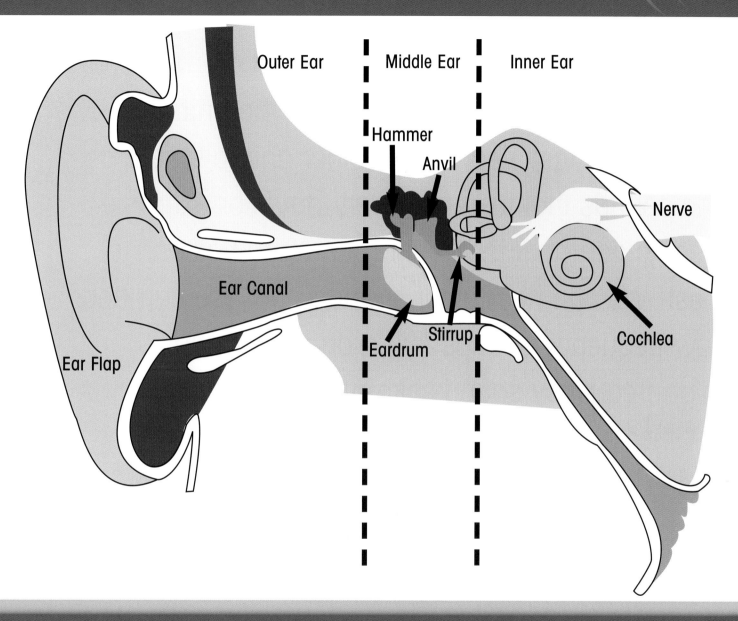

Outer Ear   Middle Ear   Inner Ear

Hammer

Anvil

Ear Canal

Nerve

Ear Flap

Stirrup

Eardrum

Cochlea

Opposite: The outside of the ear is called the ear flap. An elephant has large ear flaps. These may help it hear sounds that are far away. The animal also uses its ear flaps to keep itself cool and to make itself look larger when it feels it is not safe. *Above:* This picture shows the parts of the human ear. Can you find the hammer, anvil, and stirrup?

Sounds We Can Hear

Animals can only hear sounds that are between certain **frequencies**. This is called the animal's **audible range**. People and other animals hear best the sounds that they use every day. For example, people can hear the sound of human voices the best. We can hear other sounds, too. We can hear low-frequency sounds like a drumbeat and high-frequency sounds like a bird singing.

Other animals have different audible ranges for many reasons. For example, it is harder to see underwater than to see on land. **Marine** animals have large audible ranges to make up for the lack of vision under water.

Dolphins, such as the ones shown here, can make and hear sounds that are above people's audible range. This means that many of the sounds they make are too high for us to hear.

Ultrasound and Infrasound

We measure frequency in the number of cycles, or vibrations, a sound wave makes in a second. We call the number of cycles in a second a **hertz** (Hz). The audible range of most people is somewhere between 20 Hz and 20,000 Hz. We can hear any sound between these two frequencies. Any frequency outside of this we cannot hear. Frequencies below 20 Hz are called **infrasound**. Frequencies above 20,000 Hz are called **ultrasound**. People have learned to use sound waves that we cannot hear for other purposes. For example, doctors use ultrasound to look at parts of the body or to treat some illnesses.

Opposite: We use infrasound to find out about natural disasters like earthquakes. During an earthquake the ground shakes or shifts position. *Above:* Bats use ultrasound to hunt for insects, or animals such as moths and beetles. Their hearing at these frequencies is so sharp that they can tell the exact place where a tiny bug is.

The Speed of Sound

If you talk to a friend standing beside you, he or she will hear you right away. If you stand across a field and shout your friend's name, your friend will not hear you as quickly. The sound must travel across the field before reaching your friend's ear. You might wonder how fast sound travels. The answer depends on where the sound is traveling. If sound is passing through air, then the speed of sound is between 331 and 350 meters (1,085–1,148 ft) per second.

Next time you listen to music or speak with a friend, think about the energy that makes it possible. Every time you make or hear a sound, you are putting energy into action!

Opposite: You would hear the sound of this metal being hammered before you would hear the men's voices. This is because sound travels faster when flowing through most solid objects, than it does through air. *Above:* As you cheer your favorite team at the football game, your voices travel through the air to reach the players on the field.

Experiments with Sound: What Is Sound?

SUPPLIES NEEDED:

plastic wrap, pan or large plastic bowl, rubber band, rice, flat metal pan, wooden spoon

Sounds are caused by vibrations. When an object vibrates, it moves the air around it. You can hear and feel vibrations. You can't see vibrations in the air, but you can see and hear the things they have an effect on, like a guitar string. Try this experiment.

Step 1 Pull a sheet of plastic wrap tightly over a cake pan or a large plastic bowl. Use a large rubber band to hold the plastic in place. You've made a drum.

Step 2 Sprinkle a spoonful of rice on top of the plastic.

Step 3 Hold a flat metal pan a little above your "drum" and tap the flat metal pan with a wooden spoon or a ruler. When you tap the pan, the metal vibrates. The vibrations move the air around the tray. When these vibrations reach the plastic, the plastic vibrates, too. When this happens, the rice moves!

Experiments with Sound: Sound Waves

Sound travels in waves. These sound waves travel through the air in all directions. Here's a way to show how sound waves work.

Step 1 Fill a sink, tub, or plastic dishpan with water. Add a few drops of food coloring. Drop a pebble into the water. What do you see? Ring-shaped waves travel out in all directions.

Step 2 Try dropping two pebbles in the water at the same time but in different places. Two pebbles make two sets of waves that pass through each other. Sound waves move like this. That's why you can hear several different kinds of sound at one time.

Glossary

anvil (AN-vul) A small bone in the middle ear that vibrates.

atoms (A-temz) The smallest parts of an element, which can exist either alone or with other elements.

audible range (AH-duh-bul RAYNJ) The sounds that a certain animal can hear.

cochlea (KO-klee-uh) A snail-shaped tube found in the inner ear.

energy (EH-nur-jee) The power to work or to act.

frequencies (FREE-kwen-seez) The numbers of waves moving in a certain space each second.

hammer (HA-mur) A small bone in the middle ear that shakes.

hertz (HURTS) A measurement of the number of vibrations in a sound wave.

infrasound (IN-frah-sownd) Sound waves less than 20 Hz.

larynx (LER-inks) The part of our throat that holds vocal cords.

marine (muh-REEN) Having to do with the sea.

matter (MA-ter) Something that has weight and takes up space.

molecules (MAH-lih-kyoolz) Two or more atoms joined together.

stirrup (STUR-up) A small bone in the middle ear that shakes.

translates (trans-LAYTS) Changes from one form into another.

ultrasound (UL-truh-sownd) Sound waves greater than 20,000 Hz.

vibration (vy-BRAY-shun) Fast movement up and down or back and forth.

vocal cords (VOH-kul KORDZ) Two small bands that reach across the voice box and move to make sounds.

Index

Web Sites

Due to the changing nature of Internet links, PowerKids Press has developed an online list of Web sites related to the subject of this book. This site is updated regularly. Please use this link to access the list:
www.powerkidslinks.com/eic/sound/